IGUANA BEACH

by kristine Franklin
illustrated by Lori Lohstoeter

Crown Publishers, Inc.
New York

For Jody, who loves
the waves.
—K. L. F.

To Ash. I carry a piece of your joy with me every
day. And to P & P. Thank you for helping me to
grow as an artist and as a person.—L. L.

Published by Crown Publishers, Inc., a Random House company, 201 East 50th Street,
New York, NY 10022

CROWN is a trademark of Crown Publishers, Inc.

http://www.randomhouse.com/

Printed in the United States of America

Library of Congress Cataloging-in-Publication Data
Franklin, Kristine L.
Iguana Beach / written by Kristine L. Franklin ; illustrated by Lori Lohstoeter.
p. cm.
Summary: Though little Reina has promised not to swim in the waves
during her first trip to the ocean, it becomes intolerable for her to
keep that promise as her cousins frolic in the water—and then
she finds a solution to her problem.
[1. Swimming—Fiction. 2. Seashore—Fiction. 3. Guatemala—Fiction.]
I. Lohstoeter, Lori, ill. II. Title.
PZ7.F859226Ig   1997   96-11951

ISBN 0-517-70900-7 (trade)
       0-517-70901-5 (lib. bdg.)

10 9 8 7 6 5 4 3 2 1

First Edition

The day Tío Benito took all the cousins to Iguana Beach, Reina begged to go along. "I've never ever seen the ocean," she cried.

"The waves are big," said Reina's mother, "and you're too small."

Reina started to sob. The cousins patted her cheeks.

"Shh, shh, little queen," they said. "Don't cry."

"I suppose I could keep an eye on her," said Tío Benito.

The cousins said they'd make sure Reina didn't bounce out of the truck. Reina crossed her heart twice and promised to stay away from the waves. Finally, her mother agreed. By the time Tío Benito started down the dusty road, Reina was smiling brightly.

"No waves," called Reina's mother.

"I promise," called Reina.

"Don't worry," called Tío Benito.

The drive to the beach was long and hot. When the truck finally stopped, Reina could hear the roar of the surf. She could smell the salty air. She peeked over the bed of the truck. Through the trees, at the edge of a glittering sandy beach, Reina saw the blue-green tropical sea for the very first time.

Rows and rows of water like foamy mountains rolled in and smashed themselves against the sand. "Look at those waves!" one of the cousins shouted. Reina stared. The waves were taller than grown-ups, longer than buses, louder than hard rain on a tin roof. So wet and exciting! Reina forgot all about her promise.

The cousins tore off their clothes and flung them in a pile on the sand. They raced to the ocean in their underwear, splashing and diving into the salty froth.

Reina slipped out of her skirt and ran, too. She ran across sand
that was so hot it burned the bottoms of her feet. She ran across
the cool, wet sand near the water and was just about to plunge in
when Tío Benito grabbed her around the middle.

"No waves for you," he said.

"But I know how to swim!" cried Reina. "Please?" Tío Benito shook his head and took Reina's hand. He led her to a blanket in the shade.

"The ocean is not like a lake," said Tío Benito. "Those waves would tumble you like a coconut. You play here by me while I read the paper." Reina's eyes filled with tears. She begged Tío Benito with her round brown eyes, but he didn't notice her sadness. He was already reading his paper.

Reina watched the cousins swim and ride the waves like dolphins. She dug a hole in the sand, halfway to Spain, until a big crab came and pinched her on the bottom.

Reina watched the cousins play tag and dive from each other's shoulders. She stacked driftwood and pretended it was a boat, until a long iguana came and stuck his slithery tongue in and out and did lizard push-ups in the sand to prove he was boss.

Reina watched the cousins hold their noses and dive for shells. She found some shells in the sand—old dried-up, broken-up, bleached ones. Reina made an R for Reina with the ugly shells.

Just then, a troop of monkeys started throwing sticks and spitting. They screeched at her from the trees. Reina left the old shells in the sand and walked down to stand where the waves licked the shore. The water crawled slowly toward her—worn-out, lazy water, left over from a wave that had broken beyond the beach. Reina wiggled her toes in the water. Wet toes weren't the same as swimming.

"Be careful," yelled the cousins. "Sharks love little toes!" They laughed and dove beneath the waves before Reina had a chance to splash them.

The water was so cool and beautiful! Reina longed to swim. She would stay away from dangerous waves. She would kick all the sharks in the nose.

Reina looked up and down the beach. No one was watching. Tío Benito dozed in the sun. Reina began to run.

Down the beach she raced, away from the cousins, away from lazy Tío Benito snoring in the sand. Far away someone called her name, "REINA!" but she didn't stop.

All the cousins were chasing her now. Tío Benito, too. Reina didn't care. She ran toward the water, toward the bright, delicious ocean water.

"Stop, Reina!" they yelled.

"You promised!" shouted Tío Benito. "You come back here right now!" Reina ran around a huge rock. She didn't care if she was breaking her promise. She held her nose and was just about to run into the beautiful water when she stopped in surprise.

The cousins ran around the rock and stopped, too. Tío Benito puffed and wheezed as he came up behind them. "Well, look at that," he said.

It was a very small lagoon. The big waves crashed against a rocky reef far away. At their feet, the water lapped gently against the shore, tumbling only the tiniest grains of sand. Reina moved toward the water. Suddenly Tío Benito's arm was around her waist.

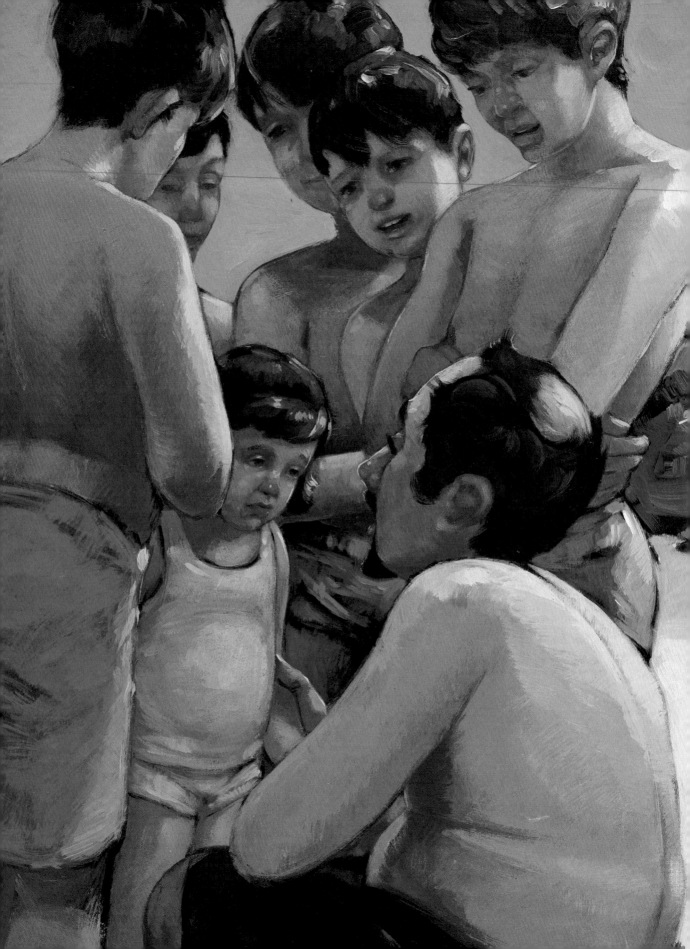

"No, my little queen," said Tío Benito sadly. "You promised to stay out of the water."

"I promised to stay out of the *waves*," said Reina.

"We don't see any waves," said the cousins. Reina and the cousins looked at Tío Benito and begged with their round brown eyes.

Tío Benito scratched his head. He looked at the water. He looked at the cousins. He looked at Reina.

"Not a single wave," said Tío Benito with a sigh and a twinkle in his eye. "I'll never finish my newspaper now." He poked Reina playfully on the nose. "Let's swim!" he yelled, and Reina and the cousins and Tío Benito all raced into the calm lagoon water together, slapping the warm sea with their hands, leaping up and flopping sideways like sailfish, dunking under and popping straight out just like dolphins.

Reina swung from Tío Benito's arms and jumped from his shoulders. She held her nose and looked for pretty shells. She splashed the cousins every time they came close. And whenever she wanted a few waves, she made them herself.